D1636179

"With *Legacy Lane*, Robin Lee Hatcher again proves why her books are so anticipated and appreciated. With this story of a woman who hits a major speed bump on her fast track to success, Robin brings us a tender story about real flesh-and-blood people, small-town neighbors with big hearts, and a mother's love."

Lorena McCourtney,
author of the Julesburg Mysteries series

"Once readers step into the engaging town of Hart's Crossing, they're hooked by the lovable residents and the warm yet thought-provoking story in *Legacy Lane* by Robin Lee Hatcher. The scenes come to life as neighbors and friends touch the lives of Angie and Francine Hunter, leading readers on a tender journey of God's amazing forgiveness and grace. Everyone will want to return to Hart's Crossing for another delightful visit."

Gail Gaymer Martin, award-winning Steeple Hill author of
The Christmas King and *Loving Care*

"Robin Lee Hatcher has a way of telling a story that makes you feel the characters are your own family. Her newest, Legacy Lane, is a wonderful story full of the warmth and charm of a Sunday afternoon in the country. Don't miss this one—you'll want to linger over each page."

Colleen Coble,
author of the Rock Harbor Mystery series

Legacy Lane

HART'S CROSSING #1

ROBIN LEE
HATCHER

Fleming H. Revell
A Division of Baker Book House Co
Grand Rapids, Michigan 49516

F
HATL

Published by Fleming H. Revell
a division of Baker Book House Company
P.O. Box 6287, Grand Rapids, MI 49516-6287
www.bakerbooks.com

Printed in the United States of America

Library of Congress Cataloging-in-Publication Data
Hatcher, Robin Lee.
    Legacy Lane / Robin Lee Hatcher.
        p.   cm.—(Hart's Crossing ; #1)
    ISBN 0-8007-1854-2
    1. Neighborhood—Fiction. 2. Friendship—Fiction. I. Title.
PS3558.A73574 L44 2004
813′.54—dc22   2003024356

To Mel and Cheryl, who have come to the medical rescue of my characters more than once. Thank you for being so willing to help.

Legacy Lane

CHAPTER ONE

Angie Hunter stared out the tiny window of the Bombardier turboprop, keeping a death grip on the armrests as the plane bounced and dropped in the turbulent air above the still, snowy-white mountain range.

Oh, how she hated flying in a tin can. Give her a first class seat in a jumbo jet any day. Not that she'd had other options when she made her flight reservations. Only regional airlines flew into the airport nearest her destination, and those airlines used small planes like this one.

Maybe she should have driven from California to Idaho. It might have been nice to have her own automobile for the next eight weeks, and the trip could have been made in an easy two days.

"Don't be silly, dear," her mother, Francine Hunter, had said when they talked last week. "I have a perfectly good car, and I won't be driving anywhere for quite some time."

I must be out of my mind.

In the seventeen years since Angie had left Idaho, she'd returned infrequently and never stayed longer than three nights at a stretch. While earning her degree, she'd taken summer jobs near the university. Part-time employees didn't get vacations, so the occasional long weekend was all she could manage back then. As an adult, she'd had the demands of her job as a reason to rush back to the city.

"I'll go stark raving mad before this is over," she whispered to her faint reflection in the window. "What have I let myself in for?"

The whine of the engines changed as the plane began its approach. Angie felt her stomach tighten.

The flight attendant, a perky twenty-something blonde in maroon Bermuda shorts and a white blouse, began her landing announcements: Fasten seat belts. Make sure seats are in fully upright position. Turn off electronic devices. Stow all luggage. No smoking until in a designated smoking area in the terminal. No mobile phones until cabin door opens. Enjoy your stay. Thanks for flying today.

With the rough air seemingly behind them, Angie loosened her grip on the armrests. The flight attendant made a final pass down the aisle. She smiled at Angie when she reached her row.

Sure, you can smile, Miss Perk. You'll be flying out again in another hour or so. I'm stuck here for the next two months!

Angie drew in a deep breath and released it slowly. She should be ashamed. After all, her mother needed her. Eight weeks wasn't going to kill her.

And it's not like I have a lot to hurry back to.

She winced at the thought.

Ten minutes later the plane touched down, quickly slowed, and taxied toward the terminal. Angie glanced out the window. The terminal was a single-story building;

there were no Jetways. The passengers of this plane would descend the narrow steps built into the cabin door, then walk across the tarmac. Thankfully, it wasn't raining.

As the plane braked to a halt, the clicking of opening seat belts filled the cabin even before the seat belt sign dimmed. Angie reached for her purse and carry-on bag beneath the seat in front of her. When she stood, she cracked her head against the overhead compartment.

Oh, how she hated these small commuter planes.

Oh, how she hated everything about her life at the moment.

Standing between John Gunn on her left and Terri and Lyssa Sampson on her right, Francine Hunter raised up on tiptoes. Her heart raced in anticipation of that first glimpse of her daughter. Francine was almost glad she was scheduled to have knee surgery. Otherwise, who knew when Angie would have found time to return to Hart's Crossing. Angie's job at her big city newspaper was important and demanding; she hadn't taken a vacation in over five years. Or was it more than six? And a serious boyfriend hadn't been in the picture for . . . Well, too long, as far as Francine was concerned.

"There she is!" Terri—Angie's friend since kindergarten—exclaimed.

Angie walked toward them, looking like a model in one of those glossy fashion magazines. She wore a sky blue silk blouse tucked into a pair of designer jeans that fit her long, slender legs like a glove. Her thick, dark hair fell loose to her shoulders, where it flipped up on the ends.

"Hi, Mom," Angie said as soon as she'd cleared the security area.

Francine kissed her daughter's cheeks, first one side, then the other. "It's so good to see you, dear. How was your flight?"

"Don't ask." Angie turned toward Terri. "I didn't expect to see you here."

"Are you kidding?" Terri replied. "I couldn't miss your homecoming."

Softly, Angie said, "It's not a homecoming, Terri. Just a visit. Just until Mom's back on her feet."

There were volumes of meaning behind those simple words that Francine wasn't meant to hear but did.

O God, she prayed, *help us find a way back to one another. Help Angie find her way to you. Make these weeks she's here with me be a new beginning for us.*

Terri glanced at the child beside her. "Angie, you remember Lyssa."

"You're kidding!" Angie's eyes widened in surprise, and she shook her head. "This can't be your daughter. She wasn't this tall the last time I saw her."

"Kids grow a lot in four years, Ang. Lyssa was five last time you breezed through town. Now she's nine." Terri softened her not-so-subtle rebuke by adding, "We miss you when we don't see you. E-mails and phone calls just aren't enough."

Francine decided now would be a good time to interrupt. "Angie, you haven't met our church's new pastor, John Gunn. Pastor, this is my daughter, Angie."

"A pleasure to meet you, Angie. Your mother has told me a lot about you."

"All good, I hope." Angie smiled politely as she shook the pastor's proffered hand. "It's nice to meet you, too."

"I offered to drive your mother down here in my SUV," John said. "She wasn't sure how much luggage you'd have and was afraid it wouldn't fit into her trunk."

"I didn't bring a lot."

Francine touched her daughter's forearm. "Well, let's go get what you did bring, shall we?" She didn't want to say so, but she needed to get off her leg. Her bad knee was throbbing something fierce.

"Ang," Terri said, "why don't you and Pastor John get your luggage while Lyssa and I take your mom to the car."

"Sure. That's fine with me."

John handed the keys to his vehicle to Terri before walking with Angie toward the baggage claim area.

"You hold on to me, Mrs. Hunter." Terri tucked Francine's hand into the crook of her arm. "We'll get you to the car and off that leg."

"Thank you, dear. I didn't want to make a fuss and spoil Angie's arrival, but I am hurting a bit." Gratefully, she leaned into Terri and allowed herself to be helped outside.

Their destination was about an hour's drive from the airport, but the time passed quickly, aided by Terri's efforts to catch Angie up on all the latest news of the folks of Hart's Crossing. As owner-operator of Terri's Tangles Beauty Salon, she was in a good position to know, perhaps even better than Bill Palmer, the editor of the local weekly newspaper, the *Mountain View Press*.

Headed toward the rugged mountain range to the north, they drove through farmland that had been reclaimed from the high desert country of southern Idaho. An abundance of horses and cows grazed in pastures turned emerald green by irrigation. Tall poplars shaded old farmhouses and barns that had been bleached over the years by the relentless summer sun.

At last, John Gunn slowed his Ford Expedition as the two-lane highway topped a rise, then spilled into Hart's Crossing's Main Street. Of course, the heart of downtown was all of three blocks long. Blink and you'd miss it.

Several people sat on benches outside the Over the Rainbow Diner, licking ice cream cones and enjoying the mild spring evening. Two women pushing strollers gazed through the window of Yvonne's Gifts and Boutique. The Apollo Movie Theater's marquee flickered and sputtered, as if it couldn't decide whether to stay on or off; Angie noticed the film they would show this Friday and Saturday was at least a decade old.

A typical Monday evening in Hart's Crossing . . . where there was nothing much to do.

"It looks the same as ever," she said softly.

John Gunn chuckled. "You'd be surprised. I think you'll find lots of changes, thanks to our mayor and the city council."

His comment irritated Angie. She was the one who'd grown up in this town, not him. She certainly knew better than he did if things were different or the same. Glancing at the driver, she said, "Well, *you're* new. I know that much."

If he thought her rude, he didn't let on. "Indeed. Relatively so, anyway."

Rather than say something she would regret later, Angie looked out the passenger window again, staring through the glass as they followed the familiar route from the center of town to her mother's home.

Eight weeks. I can survive anything for eight weeks.

CHAPTER TWO

Angie panicked when she saw sunlight filtering through the curtains. She'd overslept. She'd be late for work.

She tossed aside the bed coverings and sat up. Only when her feet touched the plush, Barbie-pink throw rug did she remember she was in her girlhood bedroom. She also remembered she no longer had a job to be late for. She'd quit last week. Packed up all her personal belongings in a cardboard box and stormed out of the building in a snit.

With a groan, she pressed the heels of her hands against her eyes. What a mess! How could everything have gone so wrong so fast?

Angie had given the *Bay City Times* 150 percent from her first day on the job. She'd routinely put in sixty, seventy, eighty hour work weeks. She hadn't taken a day off or called in sick in years. Social life? Forget it. She had none. She couldn't remember the name of her last boyfriend. She'd eaten, slept, and breathed the newspaper. But she'd been willing to sacrifice anything and everything, especially after she'd been promised Mr. Stattner's position at the paper when he retired as city editor.

Well, not promised but given reason to believe. It was what she'd worked toward for more than a decade.

Last week, she'd been passed over by management. They'd given the position to Brad Wentworth—that was the last straw. When Brad "The Jerk" Wentworth was made city editor over her, she was outta there.

Brad actually had the nerve to call and ask her to reconsider. "Come in tomorrow and let's talk, Angie. Don't throw away your career over this. There'll be other openings down the road."

"I can't," she'd told him. "My mother is scheduled for surgery, and I'm flying to Idaho on Monday to be with her while she recovers."

Of course, she hadn't *planned* to come back to Hart's Crossing. Not at first. What she'd really meant to do was hire a nurse for the duration of her mother's convalescence. But losing that promotion had changed everything, and now here she was.

Angie stood and reached for her robe. If she wasn't mistaken, the scent of coffee brewing was wafting through her bedroom door. She padded down the stairs on bare feet in search of her morning dose of caffeine.

Angie found her mother seated at the kitchen table, reading the latest edition of the *Mountain View Press*. "Morning, Mom," she mumbled, making a beeline for the mug tree beside the coffeepot.

"Good morning, dear. I didn't expect you to be up this early. Would you like me to make you some breakfast?"

"No, thanks. I rarely eat this early."

"Not good for you, you know." Her mother folded the paper and set it on the table. "As hard as you work

21

and as many hours as you put in at that office every day, you need to start off the day right."

"Well, I'm not putting in a lot of hours at the office now." Angie turned, leaned her backside against the counter, and took her first sip. "Mmm. What's your secret? You've always made the best coffee. You could charge over four bucks a cup for this where I live."

"Thank you, dear, but there's really no secret to it. I just follow the directions on the coffeemaker." Her mother smiled and released a happy-sounding sigh. "Oh, it's so good to have you home again."

Home again . . .

Angie let her gaze roam around the kitchen. It hadn't changed much through the years. It was still painted bright yellow, and as always, there were white and yellow curtains at the window over the sink, although the pattern was different from what she remembered. The Formica table with its chrome legs and the matching chairs with their plastic-covered seats and backs, straight out of the fifties, were like old friends. The mixer and mixing bowl on the counter were the same ones her mother had used when Angie was growing up. So were the canisters and the Princess wall phone.

Francine Hunter didn't throw away much.

Unlike her daughter, who was a card-carrying member of the use and discard generation.

Or I was until last week. That could all change if I don't find the right job at the right salary.

But that was unlikely. Angie had an excellent work history and all the right qualifications. She would probably find a new job before she'd even used up her accumulated vacation days. All she needed to do while she was here in Hart's Crossing was search the Internet for openings and send out resumes.

"Is there anything special you'd like to do today?" her mother asked, drawing Angie from her thoughts.

"Not particularly." The day stretched before her like an eternity. When was the last time she'd had nothing scheduled in her day planner? She wasn't much good at being idle. Actually, she wasn't much good at relaxing. Period.

"Why don't you call Terri and see if the two of you can go to lunch? She takes Mondays and Tuesdays off from the salon, and Lyssa will be in school. You should enjoy yourself for a couple of days before my surgery. After that, you'll have your hands full."

Angie swept the hair back from her face with one hand. "Yeah, maybe I'll do that. Are you sure you don't mind?"

"Of course not, dear. I'll have your company for the next eight weeks." She smiled again. "And I'm so thankful to the Lord for that."

Angie nodded as she turned to pour herself another cup of coffee. She'd learned it was better to remain silent when her mother started talking about God.

Lord, Francine prayed as she stared at her daughter's back, *please break down that wall. It's been up between us for much too long.*

Francine's memories of Angie's early childhood years were happy ones. Her husband, Ned, had been an insurance salesman. An excellent one, too. He'd loved what he did, loved helping people plan for secure futures. Francine had been a stay-at-home mom, leading Brownies and driving her daughter to piano lessons and dance lessons and baking cookies for the baked food drives. They'd taken a two-week family vacation every summer. One year it was to the Pacific coast, another year to the Atlantic. They'd seen Mount Rushmore and Niagara Falls and Bryce Canyon and the mighty Mississippi River from one end to the other.

Ned had died in a car accident when Angie was twelve. The years that immediately followed had been hard for mother and daughter. Not financially, for Ned had provided well for his loved ones, a fine example of a man practicing what he preached. But emotionally, they'd walked a difficult path, dealing with grief combined with the normal stresses that came with a girl's teenage years.

Then, at the age of forty-four, Francine Hunter had fallen in love with Jesus, and it had changed her forever. The Hunters had been a churchgoing family, like most folks in Hart's Crossing, but Francine had suddenly discovered Jesus wasn't merely an example for her to live by, that the words in the Bible weren't just good stories. Jesus was real and he was alive and he loved her. Loved her so much he not only died for her but rose for her.

Once Francine had "seen the light" for herself, she'd tried to make her daughter see it, too. She'd preached

at her and prayed over her and tried to fix her in countless ways—the majority of them wrong ways. She'd
pushed and shoved and offended. She'd cajoled and
lectured. Her heart had been right, but her actions
had been all wrong.

And in her zeal for Jesus, she'd driven her daughter
away, first from the church and then from Francine
herself.

*Oh, Lord, make her hungry for you. I don't care how. Just
make her hungry.*

The homes in the Hunter neighborhood had been
built in the early 1900s. Most of them were two stories
with front porches—some screened-in, some open-
air—but each house had a distinct personality all its
own. The front yards were small patches of green, cut
short by the sidewalk, a sidewalk rippled in places by
the roots of the large maple trees that lined both sides
of the street.

As Angie walked toward town later that morning,
she remembered the many times she'd ridden her bi-

cycle along this tree-shaded thoroughfare or skated down this sidewalk, trying her best to avoid the cracks and breaks in the cement. Terri Sampson—her last name had been Moser then—had lived across the street, and she and Angie had been inseparable. They'd had campouts and slumber parties. They'd gone swimming together and ridden horses together and, as crazy teenagers, skipped school together. And they'd pulled more pranks on unsuspecting family members and friends than either of them could count.

Angie smiled at the memories.

"Angie Hunter? Is that you?"

She halted and looked toward the street. A white Jeep had stopped, and the driver, an attractive woman with short brown hair, leaned out the window, grinning broadly. She looked familiar but . . .

"It's Cathy Lambert. Used to be Cathy Foster."

"Cathy Foster?" Angie echoed. "Good grief. I don't believe it." She walked toward the Jeep. "How long has it been?"

"Since high school graduation. Why don't you come to the class reunions?"

Angie shrugged but ignored the question. "Are you visiting your folks?"

"No, my husband and I live here now." Cathy cut the engine, obviously unconcerned about interrupting traffic by parking in the middle of the street.

"You moved back to Hart's Crossing? But I heard you were living in the east somewhere. Boston, wasn't it?"

"No, Philadelphia. That's where my husband is from. But with our kids getting older, I convinced Clay to give my hometown a try. It's a better environment for raising a family."

Angie supposed she should know Cathy had children. Her mother had probably told her when each one was born.

"So what finally brought you for a visit, Angie?"

"Mom's having surgery. I'm going to look after her for a couple of months."

"A couple months? But that's wonderful. Clay and I will have you over for a barbecue. I'd love for you to meet him and the kids. Cait's a young woman at fifteen and Cassidy just turned thirteen. I told Cory he doesn't get to grow up as fast as his sisters have."

Clay. Cait. Cassidy. Cory. Angie's head was swimming. "And how old is Cory?"

"Seven, and he's all boy." Cathy glanced at her wristwatch. "Oh no. I'm going to be late for my next appointment. Gotta run." She started the Jeep. "I'll give you a call at your mom's."

Angie stepped back, and Cathy drove away, waving out the window as she went.

"Cathy and her husband are dentists," Terri told Angie as they settled into a booth at the Over the Rainbow Diner. "But you knew that, right? When they moved to Hart's Crossing, they built a new office right next to the medical clinic. Sawtooth Dentistry." She laughed. "They named it after the mountain range, but I still think it sounds funny."

"She's the last person I thought would move back to Hart's Crossing."

"No, Ang. You're the last person anybody'd think that of." Terri leaned forward, her smile fading. "But I'd love to see it happen. How about it? Aren't you ready to give up that crazy career of yours and settle down? Get married and have a family like the rest of us?"

"It's tough to get married if I can't find the right guy."

"Have you been looking?"

Angie raised an eyebrow. "Have you?"

Terri simply smiled again. "You bet I'm looking."

"After what Vic did to you, I wouldn't think you'd ever want—"

Terri touched the back of Angie's hand, then shook her head.

"Sorry," Angie said softly.

"Remember that old Osmond tune, 'One Bad Apple'? Well, it's true, Ang. One bad apple doesn't spoil the whole bunch. Vic was Vic. He cheated on me, and it hurt when he left us." Terri gave her head another slow shake. "It hurts even more that he hasn't made any effort to contact Lyssa in over six years." She leaned toward Angie. "But the Lord's looking out for us. I hope I can find the right guy, the one God means for me to marry. One day, I hope Prince Charming will ride into town and sweep me off my feet." She grinned. "There. I said it. I'm a romantic. Go on and make fun of me."

Angie didn't feel like making fun of her friend. In fact, she felt somewhat envious of Terri's hopes for the future, although she wouldn't admit it aloud. Thankfully, Nancy Raney arrived, putting an end to their conversation.

"How are you girls?" Nancy asked as she slipped an order pad and pen from the pocket of her pastel-striped apron. Then to Angie, she said, "Real nice to see you back in town."

"Thanks, Nancy."

"You two know what you want?"

"I'll have a cheeseburger," Terri answered. "With fries and a Diet Coke."

"Sounds good." Angie knew she'd regret it next time she got on the scales. But hey, she didn't have a job—or a man—to stay thin for. "Make mine the same, with a slice of lemon in the Diet Coke."

"Gotcha. I'll bring your drinks right out." Nancy turned and headed for the kitchen.

"So," Terri said, "how will that paper survive without you for the next eight weeks?"

Angie shredded the edge of her paper napkin. "They'll have to do it for longer than that." She glanced up. "I quit last week."

Terri's eyes widened. "You quit?"

"Yeah."

"Your mom didn't say a word."

"Mom doesn't know. I haven't told her. She thinks I'm using up some of my vacation." Angie shrugged. "It's sort of the truth. I am drawing my vacation pay. I had a lot of time saved up."

"Wow. I don't know what to say. I'm shocked."

"Me, too. I haven't been unemployed since I was a teenager."

"Well, at least now you can stay in Hart's Crossing a little longer. Take some time to relax a bit. Hey, maybe you could stay for good."

"Stay?" Angie leaned her back against the upholstered booth. "And do what? What would I do around here for employment?"

"I don't know. Get a job reporting for the *Press*. Write that novel you used to talk about all the time. Flip burgers at the drive-in if you had to."

"Very funny."

Terri's voice softened. "I wasn't trying to be funny. Give it some thought, will you? You belong here. I don't think you've been truly happy since the day you moved away."

CHAPTER THREE

*I**don't think you've been truly happy since the day you moved away."*

What an absurd thing for Terri to say. Angie had been very happy since leaving Hart's Crossing. She'd gone to college. She'd excelled in her career. She'd experienced exciting things and seen exciting places during the years she'd worked as a foreign correspondent, and she loved absolutely everything about big city living.

Well, maybe not the traffic during commute hours, but everything else.

Well, maybe not *everything* else, but almost.

"At least I could get a skinny vanilla latte whenever I wanted one," she muttered the next morning as she stared at the coffeemaker, impatiently waiting for the brewing cycle to end.

"What was that, dear?"

"Nothing, Mom. Just talking to myself."

Francine Hunter chuckled. "You're much too young for that habit."

"Not really."

"Perhaps it's the writer in you. You've always had a creative spirit. Always had so much going on inside that head of yours. You're like your father in that regard, and he used to talk to himself all the time."

"Did he?" Angie filled two ceramic mugs with coffee and carried them to the table, setting one in front of her mother. "There you go."

"Thanks, dear." Her mother added a spoonful of sugar and stirred it. "What's on your agenda for the day?"

"I'm not sure. I guess I'll do some work on the Internet if you don't mind me tying up the phone line for a while." She tapped a fingernail against the tabletop. "Maybe I should order cable service."

"Heavens, no!" Her mother shot her a horrified look. "There's nothing worth watching on the channels we have now. Why pay for more worthless shows?"

"I meant cable Internet service. It won't tie up the phone line when I'm on the computer, and it's about twenty times faster than most dial-ups."

"Fast. Faster. Fastest. Everybody's in such a hurry these days." Francine took a sip of coffee. After a moment she said, "How difficult it must be for today's generation to obey the Scripture that says, 'Be still, and know that I am God.' Nobody seems to know how to be still anymore. Everyone's so busy . . . What's the term that means a person's trying to do about six things at once?"

"I think you mean multitasking."

"Yes, that's it. Multitasking. It's a dreadful word, isn't it?"

Angie opened her mouth to disagree, then closed it again. Maybe her mother was right. Maybe it was a dreadful word. Just because she'd spent the past seventeen years multitasking every part of her life didn't mean it was a good thing.

37

"I don't think you've been truly happy since the day you moved away."

"Dear," Francine said, interrupting Angie's thoughts, "you do whatever you wish about the cable thing. I'm sure you'll need to check in with your office occasionally, and if cable or whatever will help you, you should have it. I don't want your stay with me to be an inconvenience to you."

Angie couldn't put it off any longer. This was the perfect opportunity to tell her mother that she was unemployed. "Mom . . . I—"

She was saved by the proverbial bell. This one, the front doorbell.

"I wonder who that could be this early in the day." Francine rose from her chair. "Excuse me while I see."

As she sipped her coffee, Angie wondered why she was reluctant to tell her mother she'd quit her job. For that matter, why was she reluctant to share much of anything about her life?

"When did we stop talking?" she whispered. Then she shook her head. "When did *I* stop talking?" Before she could seek an answer to those questions, her mother returned, followed by their visitor.

"Look who's come to see you, Angie."

Peeking around Francine's back, Till Hart grinned, the smile deepening the creases in her wizened face. "Land sakes alive. Aren't you a sight for sore eyes?"

Till Hart, petite and spry at seventy-five years old, was the never-married granddaughter of the town's founding father. She was the sort of person who'd never known a stranger, especially not in Hart's Crossing. She, in turn, was beloved by everyone who knew her.

"Miss Hart." Angie got to her feet. She was about to offer her hand, but before she could, Till stepped forward and embraced her.

"It's been too long since you've been home." After a second tight squeeze—the woman was surprisingly strong for one so slight in stature and advanced in years—Till released her and stepped back, searching Angie's face with her gaze. "Too long." She lowered her voice. "Your mother misses you, you know. Use this time well. We can never get yesterday back. Take it from someone who's wasted a yesterday or two."

Angie felt a sting of guilt.

Francine stepped toward the kitchen counter. "Till, would you like some coffee?"

"No, thank you, Frani. I'm out for my morning constitutional, and I mustn't stay. I just wanted to say hello to your daughter while I was in the neighborhood." She patted Angie's shoulder. "You come see me, and we'll have ourselves a nice chat." As sweetly spoken as the words were, they seemed more command than invitation.

"I will, Miss Hart."

"Good. Well, I'm off." She flicked a hand in the air, half-wave, half-salute, then turned and headed for the front door, calling behind her, "Don't forget your promise, Angie. You come see me." Seconds later, the front door closed behind her.

Francine chuckled as she settled onto her chair once again. "I swear, Till's a force of nature. She'll never change."

Angie was strangely comforted by her mother's comment. She didn't want Miss Hart to change. Then she realized she was equally as comforted by the belief that her mother would never change either.

How surprising.

Terri marked off another day on the list. "That takes care of three weeks of meals for the Hunters," she told Anne Gunn. "One more week should do it."

Anne, the pastor's wife, arched an eyebrow as she leaned back in her chair. "How much food do you think two women will eat? You may be overplanning a bit."

"Hmm. Maybe you're right. As thin as Angie is, she won't eat much, and Francine isn't likely to have a large appetite right after surgery. Maybe I should start over, plan for meals to be delivered every other day."

Anne nodded. "I think so."

Terri ripped off the yellow sheet of paper from the pad and drew a new grid. Then she began rearranging the names and dates.

"I'm looking forward to meeting Angie at church on Sunday. I've heard a lot about her from her mother since we came to Hart's Crossing." Anne turned her glass of iced tea in a circle between her fingers. "John said she and Francine will drive down to Twin Falls Sunday afternoon so they can be at the hospital early Monday morning."

"I wouldn't count on Angie being in church, Anne."

"Why not?"

Terri looked at the pastor's wife. "She says religion isn't for her." Seeing the questions in Anne's eyes, she gave a little shrug and set down her pen. "Lots of reasons, I suppose. Mostly, she's too busy for God. She's very self-sufficient and likes to be in control. Besides, she's always thought her mom went off the deep end back when we were in high school. Francine *was* a changed woman after she accepted Christ."

"As we all are. Or at least we're supposed to be."

"Yes." Terri nodded, remembering the moment she gave her heart to the Lord and how the whole world seemed to change in an instant. "But Francine . . . Well, she was determined her daughter would see the light. She sort of hit Angie over the head with the gospel on a regular basis."

"Ah."

"A year or so later, Angie left home for college. By then, she'd closed her mind to anything her mom said about her faith. It's created a tension between them ever since." She picked up her pen again. "I keep praying Angie will come to understand that Christianity isn't about a religion but about a relationship with

Jesus. The same way I did." She smiled. "No doubt she thinks I went off the deep end, too."

Anne Gunn returned the smile. "No doubt."

While Angie was at the market, buying a few grocery and sundry items, Francine climbed the stairs slowly, carrying a stack of folded towels in her arms. After placing them in the linen closet in the upstairs bathroom, she went to Angie's bedroom, pausing in the open doorway. The room was tidy, the bed made, the desk and dresser tops free of clutter. In truth, there was little evidence anyone was staying in the room except for the suitcases tucked underneath the bed, peeking from beneath the pink and white gingham bed skirt.

Of course, her daughter's room hadn't always been this neat. Angie had been a typical teenager in most regards. Posters on the walls. Loud music blaring from her stereo or boom box or whatever the kids had called them back in those days. Clothes scattered on the floor, despite Francine's relentless nagging.

She sighed as her thoughts drifted back through time, back before Angie's teenage years, back to when Francine's husband was still living and their daughter was carefree. They'd been a happy family, signs of affection displayed frequently and for all to see. Angie had been a delightful child, well-mannered and cheerful and eager to please.

Things had begun to change with Angie following Ned's death, but Francine didn't know how much of what went on had been the norm for teenagers and how much had been in reaction to losing her dad.

Thank you, Lord, for the years of love Angie and I shared with her father. I can't understand what Ned's death may have accomplished in your eternal plan, but I know you never waste a hurt. Please help Angie catch a glimpse of eternity in these weeks she's at home with me.

She turned away from the bedroom and started down the stairs, holding onto the handrail as she went.

And Lord, if it wouldn't be asking too much, I would so love to see Angie happily married and providing me a grandchild or two.

CHAPTER FOUR

On Thursday, Angie phoned in the order for a cable Internet connection. The installer would come out the next morning to do the wiring, she was told. This surprised her. She'd expected to have to wait a week or more.

Excited by the prospect of being able to start her job hunt earlier than anticipated, she set up her laptop and portable printer on the desk in her bedroom, the one she'd used in high school. Oh, the things that old desk had seen. Many a night she'd opened her diary and poured out her dreams onto its pages, writing in bold, bright colors. She'd written about places she wanted to visit and things she wanted to accomplish. She'd even written about the sort of man she would one day marry.

She shook her head. Now there was a pipe dream. All the good men had been gone long before she started looking. She'd wanted to be established in her career before she contemplated marriage, but then . . .

Feeling suddenly restless, she grabbed her purse from the top of her dresser and left the bedroom. She found her mother dozing in the easy chair in the living room. Not wanting to wake her, she turned to leave.

"What is it, dear?" Francine asked softly.

"Sorry, Mom. Didn't mean to disturb you."

"You didn't. I was only resting my eyes. Did you need something?"

"No. I'm going into town to buy some printer paper. Do you want me to pick anything up?"

Francine shook her head as her eyes drifted closed again. "No, thank you, dear." She drew a deep breath and let it out. "I put the car keys on the rack beside the back door."

"I think I'll walk. I need the exercise."

"Whatever you like, dear."

Angie realized suddenly that her mother looked her age. Not old, exactly, but aging. Unlike the sixty-something women of Angie's acquaintance who had their faces lifted and peeled on a regular basis, Francine Hunter looked . . . natural. Normal. Comfortable in her own skin.

Peaceful.

Angie felt an odd tug at her heart. For a moment, she was tempted to explore the feeling, to see what had caused it and what it might mean. But she didn't. Introspection and self-analyzing were for people who had little else to do with their time. Angie was a woman of action, always busy. Always.

She quickly left the house, almost as if pursued.

Angie's trip to the drugstore—the most likely place in town to find the office supplies she wanted—took her past the elementary school, the Big Burger Drive-In, the Elk's Lodge, Suds Bar and Grill, Tin Pan Alley Bowling Lanes, Smith's Market, Hart's Crossing Community Church, Shepherd of the Valley Lutheran Church, White Cloud Medical Clinic, Sawtooth Dentistry, and both the junior and senior high schools. Angie managed to make it all that way without anyone stopping to say how good it was to see her back in town.

Her luck didn't last once she was inside Main Street Drug. She turned a corner into an aisle and ran right into Bill Palmer. Literally.

"Whoa!" he said as he grabbed her shoulders to steady her. A moment later, his brown eyes widened. "Angie?"

"Hello, Bill." She took a step back. "How are you?"

"I'm great." He looked her up and down, his gaze not discourteous but definitely intent. "No need to ask how you're doing. You look fabulous."

A flush warmed her cheeks. "Thanks."

As a freshman in high school, Angie'd had a bad crush on Bill Palmer, the handsome senior class president. From afar, of course. He hadn't known she existed.

"I heard you were in town to look after your mom while she's recuperating. The surgery's next Monday, right?"

"Yes." *I guess nothing's ever private in a place like Hart's Crossing.*

She didn't know the half of it.

"I heard Brad Wentworth got the city editor position at the *Bay City Times*."

Angie felt the color drain from her face. "How did you know that?"

"It's a small world. E-mails zip across the country in seconds. Editors talk."

She released a soft groan.

"Yeah. That's how I feel about Wentworth. I've met him several times over the years, and I think he's kind of a . . . Well, he's sort of a . . ."

"A jerk," she finished.

Bill laughed so loud everyone in the store turned their heads. "Exactly the word I was looking for," he said when he brought his mirth under control and could speak again. Then he lowered his voice. "Do you think you'll be able to work with him, feeling the way you do?"

"No." She drew a deep breath. "I quit before coming here."

This was information Bill hadn't gleaned through his editorial network. His surprised expression told her so. She found some satisfaction in that, at least.

He recovered quickly enough. "Ever think of working for a small town paper?" His mouth curved into a grin. "I could put you to work at the *Press*."

Funny. Working for a small town newspaper like the *Mountain View Press* was the absolute last thing Angie had ever wanted to do. But right then she couldn't for the life of her remember why.

Bill Palmer looked into Angie's gold-flecked hazel eyes and suspected he was a goner. It wasn't as if he'd never looked into them before. He'd grown up in this town with Angie, had seen her at community functions while they were still in school, and had run into her on her infrequent visits to see her mother after she'd left home. But suddenly, standing there in aisle four of Main Street Drug, Bill *really* saw her.

For one moment, he thought he detected a glimmer of interest in her eyes, but then she told him she had to hurry back home. Something about lots of work awaiting her. Then she grabbed a ream of paper off a nearby shelf, said good-bye, and hurried away.

Wow! What do you think, Lord?

Bill's closest friends knew he was a romantic, and in a town the size of Hart's Crossing, he doubted there was anyone who didn't know he'd like to marry and have kids of his own. But even more than that, he wanted to marry the right woman. He wanted a marriage that was blessed by God. So he'd waited. Most of the time, he'd even waited patiently. Not always but mostly.

Something in his heart told him his waiting might be over.

Terri Sampson stood in front of the mirror and stared at her reflection as she swept her curly red hair off her neck. As summer approached, it was tempting to cut it short. But she wouldn't. Short hair made her resemble a wire brush that had gone to rust.

The bell over the salon door jingled, and Terri released her hair and turned, thinking her next appointment had arrived early. But it was Bill Palmer.

"Hey," she said in greeting.

"Hey, yourself."

After Terri's husband had left her and their divorce was final—more than five years ago now—mutual friends had encouraged the never-married Bill to ask Terri out. Of course she'd said yes when he finally did. After all, Bill was funny and thoughtful, not to mention handsome. What woman wouldn't want to go out with him? But they'd both known on the first date that romance wasn't in their future. However, they'd found the next best thing—a close friendship.

"How's the beauty business?" he asked.

"Beautiful. How's the word business?"

"Wordy."

Bill made his way to the back room and returned a short while later with an open pop can in hand.

"Help yourself," Terri said, grinning.

He took a swig. "Don't mind if I do. Thanks."

Terri sat in the styling chair and gave it a shove with one foot, spinning it around one time.

"Slow day?" Bill asked as he perched on the edge of the dryer chair, forearms resting on his thighs.

"A little. I've got about thirty minutes until my next appointment. You?"

"Finished my last article an hour ago." He took another drink of soda. "Guess who I ran into over at the drugstore earlier today? Angie Hunter."

Terri cocked an eyebrow.

"Has she always been this pretty? Or have I been comatose for the past two decades?"

Bill . . . and Angie? Hmm. What could be more perfect than to have her two favorite people in the world find love with each other? Except that Angie hated Hart's Crossing and Bill loved it. And besides, Bill had a strong Christian faith and Angie . . . Well, Angie didn't.

"Did you know she quit her job at the *Bay City Times?*" Bill asked.

"Yes. She told me."

"I hinted she might want to come to work for me at the *Press*. I'd be happy to give her a column or let her cover the news."

"Bill . . . that isn't likely to happen, you know. Angie's never wanted to move back to a small town."

"People's wants can change."

"They can." She wondered if she should say anything more, if she should mention that Angie wasn't a Christian. No, she decided. This was definitely something she shouldn't interfere in, friend or no. She'd been praying for Angie to find faith in Christ, and she'd been praying for Bill to find a wife. Perhaps God was working to answer both of those prayers in one fell swoop.

Angie had expected, when she finally told her mother about quitting her job, that Francine would pressure her to stay in Hart's Crossing longer than the agreed-upon eight weeks. She'd also expected, in one way or another, to hear an "I told you so."

Instead, her mother said, "Well, dear, I'll ask God to give you a job that you'll love, one that will bring you pleasure, even more than the old one did."

"Do you think God cares what sort of job I have, Mom?" She'd meant it to be one of her usual flip responses, the sort she used whenever her mother brought up her religious beliefs. Oddly enough, it didn't sound or feel flip when it came out of her mouth.

Francine turned from the stove, where she was frying chicken in a large skillet. "Oh, Angie. He cares infinitely more than you could imagine."

"It seems to me he's got lots more serious things to worry about. Wars and famine, for instance."

Her mother set the lid on the frying pan, then joined Angie at the table. Her expression was earnest and tender. "Honey, God knows everything about you. He created you to be just who you are, with all of your unique talents and abilities. He knows the very number of hairs on your head. Of course he cares about the job you'll have next. He wants to use you in it. He wants you to fulfill your purpose in life."

Angie felt something heavy pressing in upon her lungs. "You believe that, don't you, Mom?"

"Yes, I really do believe that. He loves you. He loves you so much he sent his Son to die for you."

"Greater love hath no man," Angie whispered, repeating aloud the words from childhood Sunday school classes that popped into her head.

Her mother reached across the tabletop and took hold of Angie's hand. "Yes." There were tears brimming in her eyes.

Angie withdrew her hand and rose from the chair. "You know how I feel about organized religion, Mom. It isn't relevant today. And how could any person know which religion is true, if one even is? There's so many to choose from."

"When you meet the living Lord, you'll know what's true."

If only Angie could believe like that . . .

But no. No, she couldn't. Wouldn't. Religion wasn't for her. It wasn't. Her life as a journalist was all about facts and irrefutable proof. How could a person prove God?

With a shake of her head, Angie turned and left the kitchen.

CHAPTER FIVE

As promised, the installer from the cable company arrived before nine on Friday morning. The guy was short, cute, young—maybe twenty-five—and had spiky platinum blond hair and startling blue eyes.

"So you're why Mrs. Hunter's finally getting cable installed," he said to Angie as she led the way to her upstairs bedroom. "Never thought I'd see the day there'd be cable in the your mom's house." When she glanced over her shoulder, he chuckled. "You don't remember me, do you, Angie?"

"Sorry. No."

"I'm Eric Bedford."

The name didn't ring a bell.

"You know the summer you lifeguarded at the pool?" As he spoke, he set down the toolbox he carried and opened the lid. "I was always splashing you and pretending to drown." He grinned. "Angie Pangie."

"Good grief. You're one of *those* bratty runts?"

"Ouch!" he said, but he nodded at the same time, his grin never fading. "I remember you calling us that. We deserved it, too."

Angie sat on the edge of her bed. "What a summer. You and your gang of friends made my job unbearable."

"Well, we did our best." Eric pointed toward the desk, where the laptop was in plain sight. "I take it this is where you want the connection."

"Please."

"The order says you're only getting Internet service. You want me to wire for cable TV while I'm at it, just in case? Won't cost any extra."

Angie couldn't imagine her mother ever deciding to pay for cable television, but she answered, "Sure. Go ahead."

He set to work. "So how long are you back for?"

"A couple of months." Strange, that didn't sound as bad as it had a few days ago. "My mom's having surgery on Monday, and I'm going to look after her while she's recuperating."

"Nothing serious, I hope."

"Her knee."

"Ah." He moved the desk away from the wall and leaned down behind it.

Angie rose from the bed. "I'll leave you to your work."

"Any dogs in the backyard?" Eric asked before she reached the bedroom door.

"No."

"Okay. Thanks."

Angie went downstairs to the kitchen, where she poured herself another cup of coffee, then she sat at the table, her thoughts drifting to the summer she was seventeen. There weren't many job opportunities for teenagers in a town the size of Hart's Crossing. Not then, and she supposed not now. She and Terri had considered themselves lucky to get jobs as lifeguards at the public swimming pool.

But Eric and his friends . . .

She smiled to herself. Maybe it hadn't been so bad. Those boys had flirted with the female lifeguards in the obnoxious ways only young boys could.

She remembered the hot summer sun baking the concrete, and the glare reflecting off the water's surface. She remembered the noise of kids at play, splashing and yelling and laughing. She remembered the mothers with their babies, and toddlers in the shallow end of the pool, and the teenage boys, darkly bronzed, showing off for the girls on the high dive.

Simpler times. A time when all her dreams had still seemed possible.

"I don't think you've been truly happy since the day you moved away."

Was Terri right? Angie wondered. Had true happiness escaped her? She'd been successful in her profession—or at least, had thought she was—but what about other parts of her life? Who were her friends, people she could call and ask to go with her to a movie or a concert or a play? What, as Terri had asked her when they talked last night, did she do for fun?

I like to run.

Running was one of the ways Angie kept fit so she would have enough energy for the long hours she put in at the newspaper. Besides, running gave her time to think about the articles she was working on.

But did running bring her happiness? Did it make her any friends?

I haven't lived in Hart's Crossing for seventeen years. Why is it the only real friend I have is still here and not where I live and work?

A frown furrowed her brows.

Am I happy the way Terri is?

Angie's friend had so little in terms of career success and financial security. Her deadbeat ex-husband had taken off with another woman and left Terri to raise their daughter alone. All she had was an ancient car, a small home with a medium-sized mortgage, and her beauty salon. And yet . . . and yet Terri was happy.

Angie pictured her friend in her mind. She remembered the way Terri smiled as she ran her hand over Lyssa's strawberry blond hair, a look of motherly pride and unquestionable joy in her eyes.

Terri was more than happy, Angie realized. Terri was content.

A wave of restlessness washed over her. Maybe she needed to go for a run now. She couldn't say she cared for the direction her thoughts had taken her. Not at all.

The Thimbleberry Quilting Club had been in existence for more than thirty years, and Francine had belonged almost from the beginning. She never missed the weekly meetings if she could help it. She loved to quilt, of course, but mostly she enjoyed the time of fellowship with the other women. Most of the quilts these women made went to people in homeless shelters and other places of need. Francine hoped having something beautiful—as well as warm—to wrap up in at night would bring someone a moment of pleasure in a time of hardship.

She looked up from her needlework to trail her gaze around the long table. There were six of them present today. Francine had invited Angie to join them, but her daughter had declined while rolling her eyes, as if to say, "You've got to be kidding."

Till Hart sat at her left, wire-rimmed reading glasses perched on the end of her nose. She was easily the most skilled of all of the quilters in the Thimbleberry Quilting Club. Not only were her fingers surprisingly agile for a woman her age, but her mind was equally nimble. She could carry on a detailed discussion on any number of topics and never miss a stitch.

Next to Till was Steph Watson. Last summer, Steph had lost her husband of more than fifty years; she'd had a rough spell of it. Francine remembered only too well what that first year of widowhood was like—but Steph seemed to be doing better now.

In the chair beside Steph was the youngest Thimbleberry, Patti Bedford. A newlywed of six weeks, Patti glowed with marital bliss. To hear her talk, her husband, Al, was perfection personified.

Ah, young love. I remember what that's like, too.

To Patti's left sat Mary Benrey, the secretary at Hart's Crossing Community Church. Mary, God bless her, was all thumbs with a needle and thread, but she remained determined to one day make beautiful quilts, and so she never gave up trying. She had the patience of a saint, even with herself.

Next to Mary was Ethel Jacobsen, the pharmacist who owned Main Street Drug. Ethel, a no-nonsense type, was frustrated beyond words over Mary Benrey's ineptitude with quilting. Patience was most definitely not Ethel's forte. So why she always chose to sit next to Mary was a mystery to Francine. Maybe she liked to be frustrated.

Turning her gaze to the quilting piece in her hand, Francine said a silent prayer of thanks to God for each woman in the group.

"Frani," Till said, breaking into her thoughts, "is Angie planning to stay at a motel near the hospital during your recovery or is she going to return to Hart's Crossing each night?"

"She hasn't decided. I don't think she's thrilled with the thought of driving my old Buick back and forth every day, but she isn't keen on staying at a motel either."

Mary said, "Well, there'll be plenty of others coming down to see you when you're ready for visitors. We could bring her if she wanted."

Francine knew her daughter was too independent for such an arrangement. Angie liked to be in control. Angie *needed* to be in control.

Why is that, Lord? What is it that drives her need to control every detail of her life? And why is she so alone?

An ache for her daughter overwhelmed Francine, and her vision suddenly blurred. She was thankful the others were too busy with their sewing to notice her tears.

Oh, Father, Angie needs you more than she needs control. She needs you more than she needs success or a fancy new car or a well-appointed home or any of the other things she fills her life with. How can I help her see that?

CHAPTER SIX

Saturday morning was cool and blustery, but the Little Leaguers were troupers. They all showed up for their regularly scheduled games with the visiting teams.

"Strike 'em out, Lyssa!" Terri shouted from her place on the sidelines.

Her daughter didn't seem to hear. Lyssa stared hard at the batter as she tugged on the brim of her baseball cap. She drew her arms in close to her chest, preparing for the pitch. Then she delivered a fastball. The batter swung . . . and missed.

"Way to go, Lyssa!" Terri jumped from her lawn chair, whistling through her teeth.

"Terri Sampson, that sound could shatter glass."

Terri turned to see Angie, a blanket draped over her arms, step up beside her chair. "You came!"

"Yes," Angie grumbled, "but I don't know how you talked me into it. It's *cold* out here."

"Pansy." Terri grinned as she returned her attention to the pitcher's mound. "Shh. Lyssa's getting ready to pitch again."

The windup.

The pitch.

Strike three.

End of inning.

Terri whistled and shouted and made a general idiot of herself.

"I never knew you liked baseball this much," Angie said when they were finally seated, Terri in her lawn chair, Angie on her blanket.

"I never used to. But I like whatever Lyssa likes, and she loves baseball. Her dream is to play in the Little League World Series."

"That's a big dream."

Terri nodded. "Yeah. Don't I know it."

"Aren't you afraid she'll be hurt if she doesn't make it?"

"Oh, sure. No mother wants her child to be disappointed. But life is often hard. I wouldn't do Lyssa any favor by trying to protect her from it. And everybody should have dreams for their future." Terri looked at Angie. "As long as Lyssa learns to trust Jesus and wants what he wants more than anything else, she'll be okay. Besides, God's willing and able to take every hurt and turn it to good in her life if she follows him."

Angie stared at Terri for several moments, then gazed toward the ball field.

Terri didn't intrude on her friend's silence. She suspected there was a great deal going on inside that pretty head.

What was with all this God talk? Angie wondered. First her mother, now Terri. The things they said, the way they said it, made their faith seem more than a religious crutch for old ladies and little children, as Angie had called it many times. Their faith seemed . . . intimate and personal.

Worse yet, listening to them made her feel as if they had something she didn't have—which was ridiculous. Angie had more money in her savings, checking, and 401k accounts than her parents had made in their lifetime. She had a college degree and a resume that spelled success. Her monthly mortgage payment was probably more than Terri made in two months in her salon. Angie might not be rich, but she certainly was able to afford the things she wanted. Even now—when she was unemployed—she was far better off than most folks in Hart's Crossing.

And yet . . .

A shout went up from the crowd. Angie looked to her left to see Terri hopping up and down, waving her arms and screaming. A quick glance at the ball field explained why. Lyssa had hit a home run.

Oh, the joy on that little girl's face as she rounded the bases and ran toward home plate. A look worth far more than a large salary or a big house.

In that moment, Angie envied Terri more than she could express.

The Hart's Crossing Cavaliers—along with their parents, grandparents, friends, and supporters—jammed the tables and booths of the diner on Main Street to celebrate their victory over their long-standing rival, the Rebel Creek Warriors. The noise level was almost deafening, and Angie wondered how she could gracefully escape without hurting Terri's or Lyssa's feelings.

"Mind if I join you?" a deep male voice asked.

Angie barely had a chance to see who was standing in the aisle before Bill Palmer slid into the booth beside her.

"Quite the game." He leaned across the table toward Lyssa. "Congratulations, champ. Anything you want to say to your fans for the next edition of the paper?"

Grinning, the girl answered, "I'm real proud of the Cavaliers. They played their hearts out today, and the whole team made this win happen. I'm real proud to be one of 'em."

Bill's gaze moved to Terri. "Have you been coaching her on what to say to the press?"

"No." Terri draped an arm around Lyssa's shoulders and gave her a hug. "But she watches ESPN. She knows how the sports stars reply in those after-game interviews."

Bill looked at Angie again. His brown eyes seemed enormous, sitting as close as he was, and his smile was completely disarming. "I'll bet Little League baseball wasn't something you covered for your paper."

"No. Never."

Bill frowned as he touched his right earlobe and said, "It's noisy in here."

Angie nodded.

"Did you want to order anything?"

She shook her head.

"Want to get out of here?"

She hesitated an instant before nodding again.

Bill looked across the table at Terri. "Mind if I steal her?"

"No. It's okay. We're going to go soon anyway." To Angie, Terri said, "I'll see you tomorrow."

Bill slipped from the booth and held out a hand to help Angie do the same. Her heart pattered like a silly schoolgirl's as she accepted his hand.

It took them several minutes to make their way to the door, what with all the back-slapping and self-congratulating and high-fiving over the day's win over the Warriors. Angie also noticed a few curious looks, warning her that she and Bill would be the subject of gossip and speculation before morning.

The silence outside the diner was most welcome after the clamor inside. Angie and Bill stopped on the sidewalk and drew in deep breaths in unison. Realizing what they'd done, they both laughed.

"I'm getting too old for that kind of racket," Bill said.

"You're not old." Nobody *old* looked like Bill Palmer, Angie thought. "Not even close."

"I'm knocking on forty's door. Remember what we thought of that age when we were twenty?"

"Forty isn't old."

"I hope not." He motioned with his hand to indicate they should start walking. "There's still a few things I'd like to do before I'm officially over the hill."

"Like what?"

"Get married and have a family, for one. Travel abroad. I've always wanted to go to Ireland. And I'd like to try my hand at writing the great American novel."

Angie smiled. "I toyed with the idea of writing a novel once."

"What stopped you?"

"Never enough time." She shrugged. "Too busy with a real job, I guess. You know how it is."

"Used to, but I'm learning the importance of focusing my life better. While there's lots of good things I can do, not all of them are part of God's plan for me. I'm trying to discern what those plans are."

More God talk. It seemed she couldn't escape it. Not even from Bill.

Dave Coble, the chief of police, drove toward them on Main Street in his white car with the HCPD seal on the doors. As he passed them, he leaned close to the open window. "Some victory, wasn't it?"

"Sure was," Bill called back.

All this fuss over a kids' baseball game. It boggled the mind. But it was a good opportunity to change the subject.

"Speaking of real jobs, Bill, you haven't heard of any openings for a city editor, have you?"

He gave her a long look before asking, "In a hurry to leave us already?"

"Not a hurry, actually." She had butterflies in her stomach again. "I promised Mom I'd stay with her for the next eight weeks. She should be well on her way to full recovery by the end of that time, and it would be nice to know where I'll be living when I leave. After all, I'll need to sell my house and ship my furniture somewhere."

"Hmm. Eight weeks." His smile came slowly. "Who knows what could happen in eight weeks?"

Her mouth went dry, and those butterflies in her stomach turned into stampeding elephants.

"Who knows?" she echoed in a whisper—completely forgetting what they'd been talking about.

CHAPTER SEVEN

There was something unnerving about seeing her mother in a hospital bed.

Watching as a nurse checked the IV in Francine's arm, Angie realized she couldn't recall a time in her life when her mother had been sick, beyond the occasional cold. Francine Hunter had always enjoyed a robust good health, but now she looked vulnerable, even frail.

"Knock, knock." John Gunn poked his head into the room. "Are you receiving visitors this morning?"

Francine's smile revealed genuine gladness. "Oh, Pastor John. Do come in. I didn't expect to see you today. You didn't have to drive all the way down here."

"I know, but I wanted to. I thought you might like prayer before they take you to surgery." He glanced toward the chair in the corner where Angie sat. "Good to see you again."

Angie nodded as she rose to her feet. "And you." She was grateful he hadn't mentioned her absence from church yesterday. She'd already felt her mother's disappointment over it.

John walked to the side of the hospital bed. He patted the back of Francine's right hand, where it lay atop the thin white blanket. "Are you feeling anxious, my friend?"

"A little."

"Remember what the Scriptures tell us, Francine. Jesus healed the sick and fulfilled the word of the Lord through Isaiah, who said, 'He took our sicknesses and removed our diseases.' And one of my favorites: 'I have told you all this so that you may have peace in me. Here on earth you will have many trials and sorrows. But take heart, because I have overcome the world.'"

Angie's mother whispered, "Praise the Lord," and visibly relaxed.

"Let's pray, shall we?" John looked at Angie again. "Care to join us?"

Even as she was about to shake her head in refusal, Angie stepped toward the opposite side of the hospital bed. She did her best not to look surprised by her own actions as she took hold of her mother's left hand.

The pastor's voice was gentle as he prayed, and yet there was something powerful—and mysterious—in the words he spoke. Angie felt them wash over, through, and around her. They shook her in an odd yet comforting way.

"Amen," John said at last, and Angie's mother echoed with a softer, "Amen."

Before Angie could form the word, a nurse announced from the doorway, "We're ready for you now, Mrs. Hunter."

Angie opened her eyes and met her mother's gaze. "I'll be right here when you get back." She bent down and kissed her on the forehead. "I . . . I love you, Mom."

"I love you, too, dear. Don't worry about a thing." Her expression was serene. "The Lord holds me in the palm of his hand."

Angie stepped backward, out of the way of the orderlies. A minute or so later, she felt a lump forming in her throat as her mother was wheeled from the room. She wished she'd said she loved her one more time.

"If you'll come with me," the nurse said, glancing between Angie and the pastor, "I'll show you where the waiting room is."

Snail-like, the minute hand inched its way with agonizing slowness around the large, white-faced clock in the waiting area. The *tick-tick-tick* of the second hand pounded in Angie's head like a sledgehammer.

Right around the moment Angie thought she might start screaming, Terri and Anne Gunn arrived. Anne went to sit beside her husband. Terri sat down next to Angie.

"Thanks for coming," Angie whispered.

Terri gave her an understanding nod as she took hold of her hand and squeezed gently.

"It seems like it's taking forever."

"I know. But she's going to be fine." Terri brushed some loose strands of hair away from Angie's face, the same way Angie had seen her do with Lyssa. "If your mother follows the doctor's orders and takes care of herself the way she's supposed to, this new knee will allow her to do things she hasn't been able to do in a long while. And she'll be able to do them without the constant pain."

Angie felt a stab of shame, realizing she had no idea what her mother hadn't been able to do because of pain. Why hadn't she asked? If not when she'd first heard her mother needed surgery, at least since she'd arrived in Idaho.

Unfortunately, she knew the answer to those questions. Prior to returning to Hart's Crossing for this temporary stay, she'd been too busy with her career to think of anyone else. Since her arrival, she'd been too busy wondering what her next job would be.

Me, me, me. My, my, my. Have I always been this self-absorbed?

"Angie?"

Pulled from her unpleasant thoughts, she looked at Terri.

"Did you get to talk with your mother's surgeon this morning?"

Angie shook her head. "The nurse said he'd see me afterward." She glanced toward the waiting room doorway, then back at Terri. "I should have insisted on a consultation with him last week. I should have asked him a lot of questions."

"Don't worry. Your mom says he's by far the best knee surgeon in the area."

Angie was tempted to ask if that was a good enough recommendation. It wasn't as if this were a big city where a person had hundreds of qualified surgeons to choose from. Maybe she should have insisted her mother come to California for a consultation and surgery. Why hadn't she thought of that before?

"Harry Raney had knee surgery two or three years ago," Terri continued, "and he said it gave him a whole new lease on life."

"Harry's a good twenty years younger than Mom."

"Speak of the dickens, look who's here. Harry and Nancy. And they've brought Bill and Miss Hart with them."

Angie was both surprised and comforted by the presence of the newcomers. She'd expected to be alone in the waiting room this morning, and instead she was surrounded by people who knew and loved her mother.

Nancy Raney sent a little wave in Angie's direction as she and her husband went to sit near the Gunns.

"Is Frani still in surgery?" Till asked as she approached Angie.

"Yes. I thought I would have heard something by now but—"

"Don't worry that pretty head of yours." The older woman patted Angie's cheek. "Our church's prayer chain has been storming the gates of heaven on your mother's behalf for weeks and especially this morning."

"Thanks," Angie answered, emotions rising in her chest and making her voice sound strange in her own ears.

"Here, Miss Hart." Terri indicated the chair on her left. "Sit beside me."

"I think I'll do just that. Then you can tell me all about the game on Saturday. I'm so sorry I missed it. I hear Lyssa was the hero of the day."

Angie watched Till Hart settle next to Terri, then turned to look toward the entrance again, just in case the doctor had come while she was distracted. Instead, she found Bill Palmer standing before her.

"How are you doing?" he asked tenderly.

"Okay." She felt the threat of tears. "I didn't know you'd be here."

He gave a little shrug, accompanied by an apologetic grin. "It was a slow news day."

A week ago, she would have said every day was a slow news day in Hart's Crossing. But now . . . now she appreciated the thoughtfulness of his sacrifice. Even a small town paper made demands on an editor.

She wondered who among the people she knew in California would do the same for her if she were having surgery? Who would gather to sit in the waiting room the way these people had gathered to wait for news of her mother? Not a soul she could think of.

"Miss Hunter?"

"Yes?" Angie was on her feet as soon as she heard the authoritative, no-nonsense voice, knowing instantly it had to be Dr. Nesbitt, her mother's orthopedic surgeon. He stood in the waiting room doorway—a man in his fifties with a square jaw and close-cropped blond hair—still wearing his hospital scrubs. She hurried across the room.

Before she could open her mouth to ask her first question, he answered it. "Everything went well. No surprises. Your mother is in recovery now." He quickly shared some technical medical information that made little sense to Angie.

"When can I see her?" she asked when Dr. Nesbitt paused.

He gave her a half smile. "The nurse will come for you as soon as your mother's alert and ready for visitors. It shouldn't be long."

As Dr. Nesbitt walked away, Angie wondered if his definition of *long* was the same as hers.

Terri came to stand beside her. "I told you everything would be fine."

"Yeah. You did." She felt almost giddy with relief as she turned toward the others in the waiting room. "Mom's okay. The surgery went fine."

"Wonderful," Till Hart said.

"Thank the Lord," John Gunn added.

Everyone smiled, and Angie felt their love for her mother spill over onto her.

CHAPTER EIGHT

For the entire week Angie's mother was in the hospital, a stream of daily visitors made the drive down from Hart's Crossing to Twin Falls. In no time at all, Francine's room was filled with cards, flowers, and balloons, so many that she was soon sharing them with others in the hospital. Whenever her mother was taken to physical therapy or for some test or another, there was someone from Hart's Crossing ready to accompany Angie to the cafeteria for a bite to eat or another cup of coffee. And there was always someone ready to tell another story about the Frani they knew and loved.

"Your mother was the most popular girl at Hart's Crossing High. Cutest thing you ever did see. I had a terrible crush on her my senior year. But once she met your father, she had eyes for nobody but Ned. Oh, those two were something, I'll tell you. And could they ever cut a rug. Once the music started, they never left the dance floor, those two."

"Remember the time Frani and Till took on the city council over the gazebo in the park? It's almost as old as the town itself, and it was a shambles. Everybody expected it to be torn down, if it didn't fall down on its own first. But Frani and Till were like dogs with a bone. They wouldn't let the members of the council rest until those repairs were made. Now it's one of the finest landmarks in our town, and I make a point to thank them every Fourth of July when we're all down there celebrating."

"Your mother has the most tender heart of any woman I know. Did you know she's been taking fresh-baked cookies to that women and children's shelter in the next county for more than a decade? Rain or shine, every week she drives over there. She reads to the little ones and comforts those women. She gives them advice when they want it, and she sits quietly with those who don't. Francine has a gift straight from God himself."

"I haven't known your mother many years, Angie, but as her pastor, I'd say Proverbs 31 would be a good description of her. Do you know that passage of Scripture? No? Let's see if I can quote some of it for you. 'She is clothed with strength and dignity, and she laughs with no fear of the future. When she speaks, her words are wise, and kindness is the rule when she gives instructions.' And then it says, 'Charm is deceptive, and beauty does not last; but a woman who fears the Lord will be greatly praised.' The way your mother loves the Lord is a real inspiration to me."

"Remember when we were kids, Ang, and your mom set up that tent in your backyard so the neighborhood girls could have a campout? She was trying to get that center post in the right spot, and the whole thing collapsed on her. We were laughing so hard we were rolling on the ground and never lifted a finger to help her. I thought for sure she'd be spittin' mad by the time she got untangled from all that canvas. My mom sure would've been, but yours just laughed along with us. She's always been a good sport."

So many stories, all told with love. So many reminders of moments Angie had forgotten or had never known at all.

As dusk settled on Hart's Crossing, Angie sat on the front porch in her mother's favorite wooden rocker, wrapped in a bulky sweater, with a soft lap blanket covering her legs and a mug of hot herbal tea held between her hands. The evening air was cool but inviting, scented with the green of newly mown lawns and the purple of lilac bushes in bloom. She was thankful for the quiet of the neighborhood after the busyness of the day and the stress of the previous week.

It was good to be home.

Home.

She allowed the idea to settle over her, accepting it as truth.

It *was* good to be home.

Angie closed her eyes as she took a sip of tea. Her mother had been discharged from the hospital earlier in the day, and now she was asleep in her bed, surrounded by some of her favorite things, including her well-used Bible, a bookcase filled to overflowing, a collection of spoons from various vacation spots she'd visited in her lifetime, and the many photos of her husband, daughter, and friends that decorated the walls, dresser, and night stand.

Angie pictured her own oversized bedroom back in California. The walls were blank except for a large painting by an up-and-coming Bay area artist that hung over a decorative fireplace. No photos cluttered any surface. No bookcase; Angie rarely had time to read for pleasure. Certainly no collection of spoons.

How sterile, she thought. If a stranger were to walk into her house, what would they discover that would tell them anything personal about Angie Hunter?

Nothing, she feared, except for her dress size.

She thought of all the visitors who had come to see her mother in the hospital. All of those people knew Francine so well. They knew her past and they knew her heart. They were connected in countless ways.

And who am I connected to? Angie wondered.

No one, really. At least, not in California. If she never went back, no one would miss her. She had already been replaced at the newspaper. Her colleagues had been only that, her colleagues. They'd eaten the occasional lunch together. They'd chatted at company Christmas parties. But Angie had never let any of them into her personal life—because she didn't have one. She'd been too focused on getting ahead, too determined to prove her value to the paper, too set on moving up one more rung on the ladder of success. She'd used her money to acquire a large house where she never entertained and a fancy car that never went anywhere except work. She had the best of everything and yet . . .

Angie opened her eyes, surprised to discover the dark of night had arrived while she was lost in thought. She set the mug of cooling tea on the floor, shoved the blanket from her lap, stood, and walked to the edge of the porch. Placing her hands on the railing, she turned her face toward the sky.

When did I lose myself? she beseeched the starry heavens.

For some inexplicable reason—at least, inexplicable to her—she recalled going to the movies with her mother to see the Cecil B. DeMille classic, *The Ten Commandments*. She'd been no more than twelve when the film came to play at the Apollo, but she remembered scenes from the movie as if she'd watched it yesterday. She remembered Moses on top of that mountain, the wind swirling about him, and she recalled the voice of God proclaiming, "Thou shalt have no other gods before me."

A breeze stirred the trees, dancing through the leafy branches. It whispered a question in Angie's heart: *What other gods have you put before him?*

Suddenly chilled, she turned and went inside.

CHAPTER NINE

Enjoying the pleasant warmth of a beautiful late spring day, Francine reclined on a lounge on the back patio, her face turned toward the afternoon sun, her eyes closed. The pain in her knee was noticeably less today, nearly three weeks postsurgery. Still, she was impatient with the recovery process, even though the physical therapist said she was right on schedule.

"Mom," Angie called from the back doorway, "can I get you anything?"

"No, thank you, dear." She turned her head on the cushion until she could see her daughter. "I'm fine for now."

"Would you like some company then?" Angie stepped outside.

"I'd love it." Francine motioned toward the patio chair next to her.

Angie walked over and sank onto the padded seat. "What a beautiful day."

"Indeed."

"Miss Hart called. She said to tell you she'd drop by around three."

Francine chuckled as she looked at her daughter. "If Till brings another covered dish, I won't be able to fit into any of my nice clothes. I'll be on a diet for the next six months if I'm not careful."

"Too true. I know I've gained a few pounds since you got out of the hospital, and there's enough food in your refrigerator to feed us both for another month or two."

Francine didn't think a few extra pounds would hurt Angie in the least, but she kept that opinion to herself.

Angie patted her stomach. "I need to start running again. I talk about it, but I never do it. I don't know why. I've always been faithful with my exercises. I think I'm getting lazy."

Lazy wasn't a word she would use to describe her daughter. Angie had worked diligently, taking care of Francine's every need, driving her to physical therapy appointments and cleaning the house and running errands and welcoming the daily round of visitors. And she'd done it all without complaint.

But the best times were when, like now, Angie came to sit with her. Oh, how blessed Francine was by these precious moments of companionship with her daughter. How she had ached for them through the years. How she would miss them after Angie went away again.

Oh, Lord, forgive me. I don't mean to feel sorry for myself. You've given us these weeks together. Let me rejoice in them while they're here.

"Mom?"

"Hmm?"

"When I was a little girl, we pretty much always went to church, didn't we? You and Daddy and me."

Francine tried not to look surprised by the question. "Yes, we did. We rarely missed a Sunday. Why do you ask?"

"Well . . . I was wondering something." Angie's gaze was fastened on some point beyond the treetops. "You've always believed in God. Right?"

Francine's pulse fluttered rapidly, like the wings of a hummingbird as it hovers near a feeder. "Yes, I've always believed in him."

"Then . . . what changed about your beliefs when I was in high school?"

Francine had longed for this moment. Now that it had come, she feared she wouldn't be able to find the right words. The Bible said to always be ready to explain her Christian hope, and she felt anything but ready. What if she said the wrong thing? What if she made matters worse? She and her daughter had been estranged for so long. What if she couldn't . . .

No one can come to me, unless the Father who sent me draws him.

As the words of Jesus whispered in her heart, Francine felt herself grow calm. The primary mistake she'd made all those years ago had been thinking it was her job, her responsibility, to bring others to a saving knowledge of Jesus, even if it took a browbeating. But it wasn't her job to convince, arm-twist, or out-debate. She was simply supposed to be ready and willing to explain her hope. Hers and hers alone.

Lord, give me the right words, the ones Angie needs to hear.

It was the pinnacle of insanity to ask her mother such a thing. Angie couldn't imagine what had possessed her to do it.

No. That wasn't true. She did know what had possessed her. Ever since that night on the porch, more than a week ago, when she'd remembered the line from that old movie, those same words had continued to repeat in her head: *"Thou shalt have no other gods before me."*

Worse still, her own subsequent question had repeated as well: *What other gods have you put before him?*

She'd tried to ignore the voice, those words, but they persisted all the same.

Perhaps if she were in her own environment, in her own place, she could have sorted it through, could have figured out why this seemed to trouble her so. But here in Hart's Crossing, in her mother's home, with people coming and going all the time, laughing and joking and sharing memories, bringing gifts and trays of food . . .

Well, it was hard to think, that's all.

"Angie," her mother said softly, ending the lengthy silence, "I believed *in* God always. From the time I was a child, I believed. But I somehow missed the part about him believing in me."

Angie looked at her mother. "I don't know what that means."

"I didn't either until I started reading my Bible. That's when God's truths began to open up to me. That's when I began to realize God wanted to be personal in my life. He wasn't way up in heaven, watching me muddle through. He was with me, and he spoke to me every day as I read from his Word."

"Every religion has its own book, Mom."

"Christianity is much more than a religion, darling, although even many who call themselves Christians fail to understand that. I did for many years." She shook her head slowly. "And the Bible is much more than a mere book. It's holy because it was written by a living God. It has the power to change people, the same way it changed me." She spoke in a quiet voice, and the strength of her belief was almost hypnotic.

Angie resisted, saying, "It's just a book written by a bunch of men thousands of years ago."

"Is it?" Her mother's eyes narrowed slightly. "Angie, you've been a journalist for many years. You deal in facts. You know how to dig for truth. Why don't you investigate to see if what I say is true? God isn't afraid of our reasoning, and he isn't surprised by our questions or our doubts. He gave you your intellect, you know. So why don't you use it?"

That was a challenge Angie hadn't expected her mother to make, and her reply was even more unexpected. "Maybe I will."

CHAPTER TEN

Shoo!" Till Hart crossed her wiry, age-wrinkled arms over her chest and stared at Angie with the determination of a drill sergeant. "Get out, young lady, and don't come back for the rest of the day. We'll see to your mother."

"But—"

"You know better than to argue with your elders. Shoo, I said."

Angie looked from Till to Steph Watson to the three other members of the Thimbleberry Quilting Club who were standing in her mother's living room, sewing baskets in hand.

Till's hand alighted on Angie's arm, and her voice softened when she spoke again. "Go on, now. You haven't had a day to yourself in nearly a month. We promise we won't let Frani do anything she shouldn't."

Angie glanced toward her mother.

"I'll be fine, dear. Go and enjoy yourself."

"If you're sure."

"I'm sure."

As Angie turned toward the stairs, Till said, "And remember. Don't come back until supper time."

Fifteen minutes later—wearing a baseball cap, a pair of comfortable Levis, a pale green T-shirt, and her white athletic shoes—Angie walked toward town, breathing in the sweet midmorning air. It felt good to get out for a while. She hadn't realized how much she'd missed having some alone time, and she was glad Till Hart had insisted. Not that she'd minded these weeks of caring for her mother. It had actually been an unexpected . . . blessing. She'd felt as if she were coming to know her mother in a new—and better—way.

"Good morning, Angie," a woman called from a driveway. "How's your mother today?"

Recognizing Liz Rue, the woman who owned Tattered Pages Bookstore, she answered, "She's doing well, Mrs. Rue."

"Tell her I'll be by to see her again soon. I received a shipment of new novels yesterday, and I know she'll want to read some of them while she's laid up. I'll bring by a few and let her choose."

"I'll tell her. Thanks."

Was there anybody in town who didn't know and care about her mother? Angie wondered.

When she walked past the elementary school a short while later, Angie remembered that today was the last day of the school year.

Lyssa must be excited. More time for baseball.

She smiled, remembering summers in Hart's Crossing when she was a kid. Long, warm days of fun. Bike rides and swimming and camping and horseback riding. It seemed to her that she'd had access to most of the back doors in town. If her mother wasn't near, someone else's mother was. What a carefree existence she'd had back then.

She wondered how Terri managed, a self-employed single mom with a deadbeat ex and no nearby relatives for backup support. Was there some sort of day care program in Hart's Crossing? Or did Lyssa have to go into the salon with her mother during the summer months? It couldn't be easy for Terri, juggling so many things while raising a daughter alone.

In contrast, all Angie had to think about was herself. She used to think hers was the perfect life. But lately . . .

"Hey, stranger."

She slowed her steps at the sound of Bill Palmer's voice. She glanced quickly at Terri's Tangles Beauty Salon, her original destination, then almost without a conscious decision, headed across the street to where Bill stood.

"How's your mom?" he asked as she approached.

"Doing well."

"Glad to hear it. Sorry I haven't been by to see her this week. I had to go out of town for a few days. But I plan to drop by tomorrow after church, if that's all right."

"We'll be there."

"Hey, if you'd like, I could come by before church and take you both with me."

Surprisingly, Angie was tempted to say yes. "Sorry. Mom doesn't think she can manage being out that much just yet. And you know my mother. If she was able, she'd be there in a flash. She doesn't like to miss church."

"I know. I'm the same way. Best day of the week, in my humble opinion."

Again she was tempted to respond, this time to tell Bill about the books she was reading. Research, she called it. She'd taken up her mother's challenge to investigate the Bible and its accuracy. Of course, she should have been using that time to look for a new job, but employment hadn't seemed such a pressing concern lately.

As if knowing her thoughts, Bill asked, "How's the job hunt going?"

Angie shrugged.

"Care to see *my* office?" He tipped his head toward the door to the newspaper.

"Sure." She smiled at him, pleased that he'd asked. "I'd love to."

Bill moved toward the door, opened it, and motioned her through. "Beauty before age."

What was it about Bill Palmer that made her so prone to blushing? Angie looked at the floor instead of him as she stepped inside.

The front office of the *Mountain View Press* was a cluttered hodgepodge of desks, bookcases, file cabinets, and heaven only knew what else that was hidden beneath stacks of papers and files. It smelled of dust, ink, and old newsprint.

Ambrosia.

"I know where everything is, too," Bill declared with a chuckle. "There's a method in my chaos."

Angie laughed with him. "Of course there is."

"Here. Let me clear off a chair for you."

In short order, Angie was seated on the opposite side of Bill's desk. She expected him to turn on his computer or check his voice mail. He did neither. Instead, he locked his hands behind his head and leaned back in his chair.

"So," he said, "besides taking care of your mom and looking for work, what are you doing with yourself? This is the first time I've seen you in town since your mom came home."

"I'm only here because of Miss Hart. She and the Thimbleberry bunch ran me out of the house. They thought I'd been too cooped up and needed some sun and exercise."

"Ah."

She glanced around the newspaper office again. "They were right."

"Care to take a drive with me into the country?"

Thump-thump. She wondered if he heard her pulse jump. *Thump-thump.*

"I'm working on an article about Kris Hickman. Remember her?"

"*Crazy* Kris?"

Bill gave her an amused look. "Yeah. That's what they called her in high school."

Embarrassed by her outburst—it hadn't been the kindest of nicknames—Angie decided against asking what sort of story he might want to write about Kris. After all, the *Mountain View Press* was a family-friendly weekly newspaper, and there wasn't anything family-friendly about Kris Hickman. At least not the girl Angie remembered. Kris had been a wild-living, rough-talking teenager who drank, smoked, and popped pills. A year older than Angie, Kris had dropped out in her junior year and ridden off to parts unknown on the back of her boyfriend's Harley.

Angie remembered the worry *that* had caused the parents in Hart's Crossing, afraid their own children might be unduly influenced.

Once again, Bill seemed to read her mind. "This is a freelance piece for a magazine I sometimes write for, and it's just the sort of story they love."

"What sort is that?"

"Come on and see for yourself. We'll only be gone a couple of hours or so, and I promise you'll find the time it takes worthwhile." He leaned forward, and there was a hint of a challenge in his brown eyes. "Maybe you'll want to write the story yourself."

Thump-thump. "Okay." *Thump-thump.*

Bill had to admit that he loved the pink-peach color that infused Angie's cheeks as she looked at him. Maybe it was male pride rearing its ugly head, but he suspected Angie hadn't blushed much in recent years. He rather liked the idea that he was the one who'd made her do it.

"I should call Mom and let her know where I'm going," Angie said, dropping her gaze toward the center of the desk. "I wouldn't want her to worry."

"Good idea." Bill pointed toward the desk on the opposite wall. "You can use that phone while I gather my notes and recorder."

He watched her rise from the chair, turn, and walk across the room. He liked the way she looked in that baseball cap, T-shirt, and Levis. He'd take that hands down over some pinstriped business suit.

Man, he had it bad. He'd fallen in love in a matter of weeks. But there were several big problems standing in the way of happiness. First, he wasn't after anything less than marriage, and he knew marriage was tough enough when both parties were believers. There was no way he'd be unequally yoked. Second, as far as he knew, Angie was still determined to return to big city newspaper work, and he just couldn't see himself in that sort of life.

God, I need you to help me out. If she's the woman you picked for me—and I just keep feeling like she is—then remove the walls that stand in the way.

Francine hung up the telephone and turned her head to find five pairs of eyes watching her.

"That was Angie. She's going somewhere with Bill Palmer. Something about a story he's working on."

"Hmm." Till resumed her sewing. "Bill and Angie. Now wouldn't they make a fine match? That would certainly give Angie a good reason to stay in Hart's Crossing."

Francine felt a flutter of hope. She didn't know a finer person than Bill Palmer. When she'd prayed for a husband for her daughter, she'd always asked God to send a mature Christian man who exemplified godly values. That certainly described Bill.

Still, her hope was mixed with concern. Angie had begun asking questions about God. She was spiritually hungry. Francine didn't want her daughter's blossoming desire for truth to take a backseat to romance.

Francine sent up a quick prayer, asking God to put a shield around Angie at the same time he was opening the eyes of her heart.

CHAPTER ELEVEN

Bill Palmer drove a 1965 red Ford Mustang convertible, the sort of car people would kill to own
in California. Bill's had belonged to his father, who'd
purchased it new when he was fresh out of college, and
both father and son had kept it in superb condition.

With her ponytailed hair whipping her cheeks, Angie
stared at the majestic mountains to the north as the Mustang—top down—sped along the deserted country road.
Bill didn't try to engage her in conversation; he seemed
content to let her lose herself in thought.

Except she wasn't thinking about anything. She was
simply enjoying *being*. Being with Bill. Being in this

convertible, sun on her face, wind in her hair. Being away from the hustle and bustle of life. No to-do list to check. No appointments to keep. No stress or worries.

After about fifteen minutes, Bill slowed the car and turned onto a single-lane gravel road. It wound into the foothills, dead-ending when it reached an old, weather-beaten, two-story house surrounded by a corral, a barn, and other outbuildings in various stages of disrepair. Two black-and-white border collies rose from the porch and barked a warning before racing out to circle the Mustang, heads slung low. They didn't look particularly ferocious, but Angie made no move to open her door, just in case.

"Lady. Prince. Get back here."

Angie looked toward the house again. A rail-thin woman with pixie-short blonde hair, wearing a faded plaid shirt and denim coveralls, stood in the front door-way of the house, her face shadowed by the porch roof. She held a toddler in the crook of one arm, balancing the child on her hip.

"Is that Kris?" Angie asked. The girl she remem-bered had been on the chunky side, and her hair had been long, reaching all the way to her waist.

"Yes, that's her." Bill opened the driver side door as he waved toward Kris. "Hope you don't mind," he called as he stood. "I brought a friend with me."

"Don't mind a bit." Kris moved to stand on the edge of the porch.

As Angie got out of the car, two things registered in her mind. First, two young girls—perhaps three and four years of age—had come out of the house to stand near Kris, each gripping one of her pant legs. Second, the right side of Kris's face bore an angry scar that pulled at the corners of her eye and mouth.

Bill met Angie at the front of the car and took hold of her arm. "This is Angie Hunter, Francine's daughter. Maybe you remember her from Hart's Crossing High." They walked together toward the foot of the porch steps.

"Well, I'll be." Kris's grin was lopsided due to the scar, but it was genuine. "It's good to see you again, Angie. I hear your mother's recovery is going well. Give her my best, will you?"

"Of course."

"Come on up and have a seat on the porch." Kris touched the head of the older of the two girls. "Ginger, can you and Lily play with your dolls while Aunt Kris visits with her guests?"

Ginger nodded but didn't budge.

Kris looked at Bill. "Would you mind taking the baby while I get the other two settled?"

"Glad to." He released Angie's arm, then handed her the steno pad and pen he'd carried in his other hand. "Come here, Tommy," he said as he climbed the three steps.

The toddler grinned and nearly sprang from Kris's arms to Bill's. It was obvious to Angie this wasn't Bill's first visit to the Hickman place. Was that jealousy she felt?

While Bill, little Tommy in arms, and Angie sat on two straight-backed chairs, Kris and the girls disappeared inside. Minutes later, they were back, Kris carrying a blanket along with several dolls and stuffed animals. She spread the blanket on the floor near a third chair and soon had Ginger and Lily seated in the center of the blanket, playing with their toys.

"Sorry," she said. "They're still pretty shy around strangers. A whole lot better now than they were six months ago, though." Softly, she added, "Thank God."

Those two words on the lips of the "crazy Kris" of Angie's memory would have sounded totally different than the way they sounded now.

"Can I get either of you something to drink? I made some sun tea yesterday."

"I'm fine," Angie answered.

"So am I," Bill echoed.

"If you're sure." Kris sat on her chair.

Bill shifted Tommy to his left thigh. "We're sure." He glanced at Angie. "You mind taking notes since I'm holding the little guy?"

She shook her head, rather glad for something to do. Otherwise, she was afraid she would stare at Kris's scar, especially now that the woman was sitting so close.

Bill reached into his shirt pocket and withdrew his tiny recorder before saying, "Kris, why don't you tell us your story in your own words? We'll save any questions until the end." He set the recorder near his interview subject and turned it on.

"Okay." Kris glanced down at the two small girls, then turned her head to gaze toward the rolling landscape. "I guess if I say I was a wild kid, it wouldn't surprise either one of you."

No, Angie thought, *it wouldn't.*

"I was using drugs and drinking pretty heavy by the time I was a sophomore. I was way more than my mom could handle, that's for sure. She was a widow by then. Trying to raise me right and take care of this place by herself was too much. When she tried to discipline me, I fought back. I was a real hellion." She took a deep breath and let it out. "Finally I took off with my boyfriend, Grant. He was both my lover and my supplier, and I needed him for both reasons. Over the next couple of years, we traveled all around the country. Wherever the wind blew us, that's where we ended up."

Kris's tale was not unlike the stories of countless other women trapped in the drug and alcohol culture. The poverty. The homeless, vagabond existence. The verbal and physical abuse that came in waves. And eventually, abandonment by the man she'd thought she loved. A succession of other men had followed, complete with reckless, meaningless sex and an increasing need for a chemical high.

"When the car accident happened—" she touched the scar on her cheek—"I was so wasted I didn't remember a thing. Still don't. I came to in a hospital in Richmond, Virginia, and they told me the driver, the man I'd been with, had been killed." There were tears in her eyes, but she blinked them away before they could fall. "The sorry thing is, I didn't even know his name. Had no idea where he'd picked me up or how long we'd been together. Days? Weeks? Months? Truth was, I didn't even know I was in Richmond until later on. So I laid there in that hospital bed, knowing I was never going to be pretty again, that I was always going to have a scarred face. I understood the mess I'd made of my life, and I saw what I'd become, and I wished God would strike me dead right then and there." Her smile, when it came, was nothing less than angelic, despite its lopsidedness. "Instead, he gave me a glimpse of heaven. It was like the walls of that hospital room slid open, like automatic doors at a department store, and Jesus was standing there, saying, 'Look what I have for you, Beloved, if you follow me.'"

Angie was transfixed by both the expression on Kris's face and by her words. She forgot about the steno pad and her note taking. She almost forgot to breathe.

"So I followed him," Kris finished softly, "and there hasn't been a day since that he hasn't made me glad for it."

Kris continued with her story, telling of the many months of her recovery, both from the accident and from her addictions. She told of the woman from a local church who took Kris into her home and nourished her with love and a foundation in her newfound faith.

"It took me over a year to work up the courage to call home. I hadn't talked to Mom since I ran away at sixteen, and I was afraid she'd never be able to forgive me. Finally I realized I had to call, whether she forgave me or not. I had to tell her how sorry I was for what I'd done to her, for the way I'd disrespected her. Only I was too late. Mom had passed away about the same time as my accident, and I never even knew it." Her voice lowered, and the tears returned to her eyes. This time she allowed them to fall. "I never got to tell her how sorry I was for what I put her through. We think there'll be plenty of time to make amends with those we love, but that isn't always true."

Kris fell silent, but Angie knew there was more to come. The evidence of that was sitting on Bill's lap as well as playing with dolls on a blanket next to Kris's chair.

"It took a while for me to work through the pain and confusion I felt. And all the guilt. I carried around a load of guilt for a long time before I laid it at the foot of the cross like Jesus tells us to. And then he sent these little ones into my life to love and to love me in return."

"You're not really their aunt," Angie said, suddenly remembering Kris was an only child, same as she was.

Kris stroked Ginger's hair. "No, I'm not. That's just what the kids call me. I became friends with Susan, their mom, in a Bible study we were in together, and later I took care of her when she was dying of cancer. She had no other family to see to her, and she wasn't married to their father. Besides, he took off when she got pregnant with Tommy. After they found her cancer, the doctors wanted her to have an abortion, said it would improve her chances of surviving longer, but she wouldn't do it. Susan said she wouldn't take his life to save her own. She went home to be with the Lord when Tommy was about five months old. Long enough for her to take care of arrangements for her children to stay with me. After we buried Susan, the kids and I moved back here, to the house Mom left me in her will. It's a miracle, really, the way God's provided for us all."

A miracle? Wouldn't a miracle have been for Susan to live instead of die of cancer? Wouldn't a miracle have been if Kris hadn't been scarred in that accident or had never run away from home in the first place?

As if Kris had heard Angie's thoughts, she said, "I didn't have anybody. They didn't have anybody. But together, we make a family. That's God's miracle. All things work together for good for those who love God and are called according to his purpose."

Angie was incredulous. "You're saying you think this all worked out for the best?"

"For the best?" Kris shook her head slowly. "No, I'm not saying that. Lots of bad, hard things happen to people, and plenty of it isn't the best. The best won't happen until this world is free of sin, once and for all, and God's will is done on earth the same way it is in heaven. But for now, he takes what the devil means for harm against us, and he turns it into something beautiful in the lives of those who trust Jesus. That's what he's promised in his Word." Kris leaned forward in her chair, her gaze so filled with peace it seemed to pierce Angie's soul. "That's how much the Lord loves us."

The old Angie—the one who'd arrived in Idaho on that small plane thirty-one days before—would have scoffed outright. She would have accused Kris Hickman of sermonizing or, at the very least, being simpleminded. But today, seeing something in this woman's eyes, hearing it in her voice, she neither scoffed nor accused. She listened, and she tried to understand. She wanted very much to understand where that sort of peace came from . . .

Because she knew she didn't have it.

CHAPTER TWELVE

Angie tossed and turned on her bed that night, unable to fall asleep, unable to shake the voice in her head and the memory of Kris Hickman and those three children, unable to ignore the peace she'd read in Kris's eyes, despite the painful nature of her story.

"I was way more than my mom could handle. . . . So I laid there in that hospital bed, knowing I was never going to be pretty again. . . . Jesus was standing there, saying, 'Look what I have for you, Beloved, if you follow me.' So I followed him. . . . I never got to tell her how sorry I was for what I put her through. We think there'll be plenty of time to make amends with those we love, but that isn't always

true. . . . It's a miracle, really, the way God's provided for us all. . . . He takes what the devil means for harm against us, and he turns it into something beautiful. . . . That's how much the Lord loves us . . .

"*That's how much the Lord loves us . . .*

"*That's how much the Lord loves us . . ."*

At 3:00 A.M., Angie gave up and got out of bed.

Tucking one leg beneath her bottom, she sat on her desk chair, opened her laptop, and turned it on, determined she would seriously begin her job search. Surely that would help cure whatever ailed her. Getting back to the real world was what she needed. Getting back to the hustle and bustle of the newspaper business.

Only instead of clicking the Internet link on her desktop, she opened her word processing program. She sat there a while, staring at the cursor blinking on the screen, and then she typed: **Kris Hickman is an unlikely heroine in a very different kind of love story.**

It wasn't a bad lead. Maybe not the best, but not bad either. And it didn't matter one way or the other since she had no intention of writing the article. It was an interesting story but had nothing to do with her.

Maybe she'd simply needed to jot down a few things in order to clear it from her head.

"I never got to tell her how sorry I was for what I put her through. We think there'll be plenty of time to make amends with those we love, but that isn't always true . . ."

Perhaps those were the words that troubled Angie most of all. What if something far worse than knee problems had affected her mother? What if she'd died without Angie seeing her again? Worse still, since her return to Hart's Crossing, had Angie admitted, even to herself, the many ways she'd neglected her mother? Oh, she'd made those occasional visits and had called on a semi-regular basis, and her day planner had helped her remember to send flowers on Mother's Day and birthday gifts every February, items purchased in haste and without much thought for whether or not they were things her mother would want or need.

But what about the one thing that really mattered? What about giving of herself, of her time? No, that she hadn't done. But what was a career woman to do? Angie had to have a job, didn't she?

Of course, Bill had offered her employment at the *Press*. The pay couldn't be much, but if she sold her house in California, she would have a nice nest egg to see her through for a long spell. Despite her dire expectations, she hadn't found these weeks in Hart's Crossing onerous. Maybe she'd even enjoyed them.

She thought of Kris Hickman again and the strength of the faith that had been revealed as she related her story. A strong faith shared by Angie's mother, Bill Palmer, and Terri Sampson, to name only a few of the people she knew. For the first time in her life, Angie wanted to know *why* they believed what they believed. Perhaps if she stayed in Hart's Crossing a while longer, she'd find the answers to the questions that plagued her.

Angie swiveled her chair around 180 degrees, thinking that her life had been a good deal simpler when she wasn't so bent on self-analysis and spiritual discovery.

Francine awakened to the smell and sound of bacon sizzling in a frying pan. Turning her head on the pillow, she looked at the red numbers on her digital clock. Six-forty. What on earth? Angie rarely ate breakfast, let alone this early in the morning.

Francine sat up and reached for her robe. A short while later, aided by her cane and moving slowly, she made her way out of her bedroom, down the hall, and into the kitchen. The table had been set with the bright yellow plates Francine favored. The clear-glass tumblers had been filled to the brim with grapefruit juice.

"My word," she said. "Are we expecting company?"

Standing at the stove, her back toward the kitchen entrance, Angie glanced over her shoulder. "Morning, Mom." She smiled at Francine as she pulled the skillet from the burner. "I thought I'd get a jump start on breakfast. Are you ready for your eggs? I can fry them now that you're up."

"Thank you, dear." Francine wasn't nearly as hungry as she was curious. "Just one egg, though." She took her usual seat at the table.

"Okay." Angie removed the strips of bacon from the frying pan and placed them on paper towels to drain before taking the eggs out of the refrigerator. "I couldn't sleep last night, Mom. I was thinking a lot about the meeting Bill and I had with Kris Hickman."

Angie hadn't said much to her mother when she'd returned home the previous afternoon, other than to say where she'd been. Francine had been careful not to press for details. She'd sensed Angie wasn't ready to talk, that she'd needed to allow what she'd heard to sink in. Now it appeared her daughter was ready to open up.

"I was thinking maybe I—" Angie stopped abruptly, pulled the skillet from the burner a second time, and turned toward Francine. "Mom, I love you."

A lump formed in Francine's throat. "I love you, too, dear."

"I . . . I need to tell you how sorry I am."

"Sorry? For what, honey?"

Angie came to the table and sat down. "I love you, Mom, but I haven't shown it the way I should. I've been so stingy with my time. I've loved you when it was convenient for me and my schedule. That's a selfish, self-centered kind of love. All these years, you've never chastised me for my selfishness, even though it must have hurt you." Tears brimmed in her daughter's eyes. "I'm so sorry."

Francine took hold of one of Angie's hands and squeezed. "You're forgiven, my darling child. I've always understood how important your career is to you."

Angie shook her head, as if denying her mother's statement. "Last night I kept thinking of how Kris Hickman never got to tell her mom she was sorry, never got to spend time with her as an adult. She never got a second chance with her mom after she ran away from home. I don't want that to happen to us. I want to be close to you, Mom."

For a time, neither woman spoke because neither of them was able. They sat in silence, holding hands, and allowed forgiveness to flow between them. Finally, Angie sniffed, rose from her chair, and went to retrieve the box of tissues on the kitchen counter near the telephone. After wiping her own eyes and blowing her nose, she brought the box to the table so Francine could make use of the tissues, too.

Francine was still dabbing at the corners of her eyes when her daughter said, "Mom . . . I think maybe I'd like to stay in Hart's Crossing a while longer. What would you say to that?"

"Oh, honey. I'd love it more than anything. You know I would."

Angie sat down again. "I don't know for how long. But I . . . Well, I need to figure out some things about myself. I need to change some of my priorities. I think I could do that better here, without the pressures of my career pulling me this way and that."

Thank you, Jesus. Oh, thank you.

"I thought I'd talk to Bill later this morning. He mentioned I could do some work for him at the *Press*. I doubt he could pay me much, but the money isn't an issue right now."

Francine had the almost irresistible urge to jump from her chair and shout "Hallelujah!" as she danced about the kitchen, bum leg or no. But she managed to maintain control of her emotions, pretending calm as she said, "You do what you think is best, dear. You're welcome to stay with me for however long you wish."

"Okay, then." Angie grinned. "Guess I'll fix the rest of our breakfast now. I'm famished."

Angie chose to walk into town later that morning. Sunlight filtered through the leafy tree branches to cast a latticework of light and shadows upon the sidewalk and street. The buzz of lawnmowers came to her from several directions. Three boys, about the same age as Lyssa, rode their bikes past her, going in the opposite direction, and all of them said "Hey" as if they knew her.

Hart's Crossing never changes.

Just a month ago, she'd thought the same thing with derision. Now she was glad for it, even while knowing it wasn't entirely true. Her hometown had changed. People had moved away. Others had arrived to make this place their home. The high school had been remodeled. The Lamberts had built their dental clinic. Hart's Crossing Community Church had a new pastor in John Gunn, and Dr. Jeff Cavanaugh had taken over the practice of old Doc Burke when he'd retired.

But Angie could still count on the wisdom of Till Hart and the juicy hamburgers at the Over the Rainbow Diner and the folksy news included in the *Mountain View Press*. She knew kids would still ride their bikes down the middle of the street and the police chief would know most folks by name and neighbors would go to hospital waiting rooms to sit with family members, whether asked or not.

Maybe in the weeks and months to come, however many that might be, she could add to her list of things that had and had not changed about Hart's Crossing.

And about herself.

Seeing the "open" sign in the door of Terri's Tangles Beauty Salon, she stopped there first. She found her friend seated in her salon chair, sipping a cup of coffee.

"Hi, Terri," she said as bells tinkled overhead.

"Well, hey. Didn't expect to see you this morning. What's up?"

"Not much."

Terri's eyes narrowed. "Then why do you look like the cat that swallowed the canary?"

"Do I?" Angie sat in a blue hard-plastic chair. "Maybe it's because I'm happy."

"Why? What's happened?"

"Maybe it's none of your business." She tried to sound irritated but failed.

"Everything's my business. I'm a hair stylist. People tell me as much as any therapist or bartender might hear." She wiggled her fingers in a spill-the-beans fashion.

Angie pushed her hair back from her face as she turned her head to look out the window. Across the street was the Hart's Crossing Municipal Building and the city park with its white gazebo near the river.

"Ang?"

Without looking at Terri, she said, "You know how lots of towns put speed bumps on certain streets when they can't get traffic to slow down the way they're supposed to?"

"Yeah."

"Well, I feel like somebody installed a giant speed bump in my life this spring." Angie turned toward her friend again. "I'm going to slow down and take a look at the neighborhood I'm passing through. Maybe I'll discover I like it more than I thought I would."

Terri leaned forward in her chair, grinning as if she already knew the answer. "And that means what, exactly?"

"It means I'm not in such a hurry to return to the rat race. It means I want to figure out what matters in this world. It means I want to spend more time with my mom so we can get to know each other again. It means I want to see more of you and Lyssa, too." *And more of Bill Palmer,* she thought, but she couldn't bring herself to speak those words aloud just yet.

"It means you're going to stay in Hart's Crossing!" Terri squealed as she jumped up from her chair.

Angie grinned. "Yeah, that's what it means. At least for now."

CHAPTER THIRTEEN

Long after darkness had blanketed Hart's Crossing,
long after the lights in the homes in the Hunter
neighborhood had winked out, long after her mother
had retired for the night, Angie sat in one of the rock-
ers on the front porch. She watched the twinkling
stars overhead and thought how they'd never seemed
so bright in the city.

What was it her mother used to say? God's in his
heaven. All's right with the world.

Tonight, Angie could believe it.

Only she didn't think he was just in his heaven. It
seemed the more Angie looked around, and the more

she was with her mother and Terri Sampson and Bill Palmer and Kris Hickman and Till Hart and John Gunn, the more she thought it was possible God was here on earth, too.

"Am I right?" she whispered. "Are you here?"

It might have been nice if he'd answered her in the same way he'd spoken to Moses in *The Ten Commandments.* Then she would have been left without a shred of doubt. But he didn't. If God listened to her soft inquiry, he didn't give her an audible reply.

Maybe he wanted her to figure it out for herself, the slow way. Maybe this was another speed bump in the road of her life.

What was it she'd read in the past few days? That it was impossible to please God without faith, and that faith was the confident assurance that what was hoped for was going to happen.

Faith in the unseen, in the hoped for. A huge request for someone with Angie's penchant for fact gathering, for trusting only in the seen and the proven. Huge but maybe not impossible.

After all, Angie thought as a strange peacefulness surrounded her, she had a legacy of faith and love—from her mother and from her friends in Hart's Crossing—to help her find the way.

"Who knows?" she said, still staring at the heavens. "Maybe you'll even see me in church tomorrow. Now wouldn't that shock the good folks of my hometown?"

Smiling in amusement, Angie rose from the rocker and went inside.

A sneak peek at Book 2 of the Hart's Crossing series

Veterans Way

PROLOGUE

August 1945

Stephanie Carlson wouldn't ever forget the jubilation that raced through Hart's Crossing, Idaho, at the end of World War II. People were dancing in the streets and blowing horns and whooping and hollering and setting off fireworks. As a nine-year-old, she couldn't quite grasp the significance of everything her parents and the other adults said, but she understood something wonderful had happened.

So did ten-year-old Jimmy Scott.

Maybe that's why he gave Stephanie her very first boy-girl kiss right there outside the Apollo Movie Theater on that warm August night. The kiss might not have been as dramatic as the photograph she would see later, the one of that sailor bending a nurse over his arm and kissing her right on the lips. But that didn't stop Stephanie's heart from racing, and it didn't stop her from deciding, then and there, that she was going to marry Jimmy Scott when she grew up.

A native Idahoan, **Robin Lee Hatcher** is the best-selling author of over forty contemporary and historical novels, including *Firstborn, Ribbon of Years,* and *The Forgiving Hour.* Her numerous recognitions include the Christy Award for Excellence in Christian Fiction (*Whispers from Yesterday*), the RITA Award for Best Inspirational Romance (*Patterns of Love* and *The Shepherd's Voice*), and the RWA Lifetime Achievement Award. Robin loves to share her passion for serving God through the written word with others and is a frequent speaker at writers' conferences and Christian women's retreats. When not writing, she revels in her roles of wife, mom, and grandma. She and her husband live in Boise with their two hyperactive dogs and one aristocratic cat.

Each spring, watch for more news from

HART'S CROSSING

the small town with the big heart